WORLD WORKPLACE

Dear Reader

Have you met children at your school who have moved from another city or country?

Every year, thousands of families move to new places around the world for work.

OUR DOGS ARE FAMILY, TOO! EVERY TIME WE MOVE TO A NEW COUNTRY, WE HAVE TO TAKE OUR DOGS WITH US!

SHARON PARSONS

In this book, many families have allowed us to tell of their lives in a world workplace.

Pets travel too, so check out Chapter 6 and you'll also meet my dog, Bibi.

I hope you enjoy reading about kids and their families moving to new places as much as I have enjoyed writing about them!

Sharon Parsons

My sincere thanks to the following people for their time, information, images and enthusiasm for this book:

Chapter 3:
Nandini, Shripad, Sonali and Sohan
Chapter 4:
Kathy Nunn and her family
Chapter 5:
Sean McBreen and his family
Chapter 6:
My dog, Bibi!

NELSON
CENGAGE Learning™
For learning solutions, visit cengage.com.au

Contents

World Workplace

TEXT TYPE
Description

6

page 23

1 Moving to a New Country

New **Jobs** and New **Homes**

Many parents change their jobs. Sometimes the family has to move to a new city or a new country. If that happens, there are a lot of changes for the family. It can be exciting and challenging.

You may know kids who are new to your school – or it may be you who has moved!

New Things to Learn

There may be many things to learn about the new country or city and its way of life. A family might make a list like this:

- research the new country – its culture and language
- visit the new country
- visit new schools
- look at new homes
- visit shops, sports clubs and community services.

new friends!

WHY **WORK AND LIVE** *IN A NEW COUNTRY?*

People move to new countries for many reasons:

- a parent's company might have asked them to work in a new country
- a parent might want to study in a new country
- people might want to live closer to their family in another country
- a parent might have found a better job in a new country.

nearly packed!

Electronic Passports

an electronic passport

An electronic passport, or e-passport, has a microchip in it. A photo of the passport-holder's face is digitally stored on the microchip. Airports using biometric technology can scan and check if the face on their database and the face on the microchip match. Many countries have been using e-passports since 2005.

2 Issues for Kids

Moving **Isn't** Easy

Moving to a new country is exciting for kids, but may not be easy. Kids may:

- miss family and friends
- miss their old home and school
- think about their new school
- try to make new friends
- need to learn a new language
- learn a new culture.

Health and Safety

Emergency Numbers

Many things that we know off by heart in our old countries have to be re-learnt in the new country. For example, if you were a New Zealand kid moving to Australia, you'd have to remember to dial 000 in emergencies, and not 111. If you were a kid from the USA moving to England, you'd have to remember to dial 999, and not 911.

000

Social Studies

Modern Nomads

A nomad is the name given to a person who travels from place to place rather than living in just one place. Some nomads travel through the desert, setting up their tents in a different place every night. Many families today are like modern nomads, moving between countries and cities to live and work.

Missing Friends

It is natural to miss friends while living in a new place. Even at a distance, kids can do many things with their friends.

Communicate: keep in touch with friends via phone, texts, emails, webcam, letters and postcards.

friends keeping in touch

making new friends

HAPPY BIRTHDAY

Remember Birthdays: send close friends a birthday card or a gift from the new country.

New School

Everyone feels a little nervous when going to a new school. Children can try to:

- ask the teacher if there are kids in the class from other cities or countries – these kids may feel the same way!
- join school sports teams and school activity clubs – that will be fun!

a happy day at a new school

Remember Special Days

While away, people celebrate special days from their home country. Here are just some of the ways people celebrate their special days.

India's flag

Indian Families: may celebrate Diwali – an Indian Festival of Lights. It is celebrated when there is a new moon between 13 October and 14 November. Diyas are lit to celebrate the victory of good over evil. Diyas are clay pots filled with coconut oil and wicks, like candles.

China's flag

Chinese Families: may celebrate Chinese New Year – the first day of the Chinese calendar. This usually happens on a full moon in February – the full moon date changes from year to year.

Ireland's flag

Irish Families: may celebrate St Patrick's Day on 17 March. Many people wear green, the colour of the shamrock leaf. But … St Patrick's colour was actually blue!

the USA's flag

Families from the USA: may celebrate Thanksgiving on the fourth Thursday of every November. Thanksgiving is a time to be thankful for food and other good things in life. Thanksgiving meals usually include roast turkey and pumpkin pie.

Greece's flag

Greek Families: may celebrate Greek Easter. The dates can change from year to year – in April or in May.

3 A Third-Culture Family

From **India** to **Australia**

Sonali and Sohan's parents, Nandini and Shripad, have lived in five countries over the past twelve years:

- India
- the United Kingdom
- the USA
- Belgium
- Australia.

Sonali has lived in Belgium and Australia.

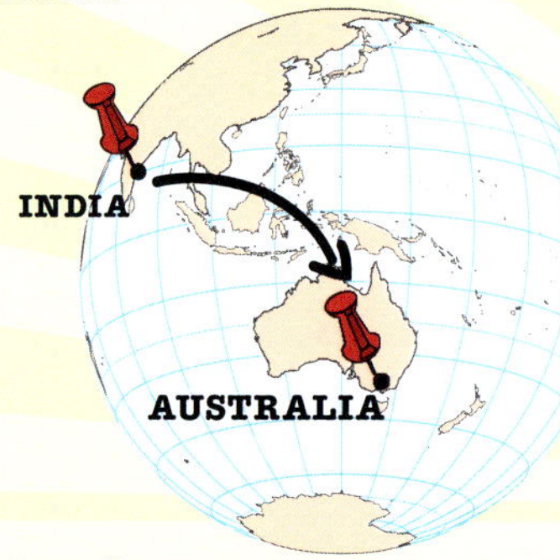

Sonali's family meet a koala for the first time.

Sonali's Dad

Sonali's dad is highly skilled in Information Technology (IT). Companies around the world want to employ him. Work is the only reason why his family has moved to several new countries.

Sonali meets a wallaby for the first time.

Who Are Third-Culture Kids? (TCKs)

“Third-Culture Kids” spend many years living in a different culture or country from either of their parents’ cultures or countries.

Take for example, a kid living in Australia with a Chinese mother and an Irish father. The kid’s first culture will be Chinese (like their mother) and their second culture will be Irish (like their father). The kid’s third culture will be Australian because this is where they spend most of their childhood.

Third-Culture Grown-Ups (TCGs)

“Third-Culture Grown-Ups” may have grown up as “Third Culture Kids”. Third-Culture Grown-Ups may better understand different cultures and be able to work well in different countries.

Sonali and Sohan's Birthplace

Sonali's family first lived in Bangalore, India, and that is where Sonali was born. But Sonali's brother Sohan was born in Australia.

Sonali and Sohan

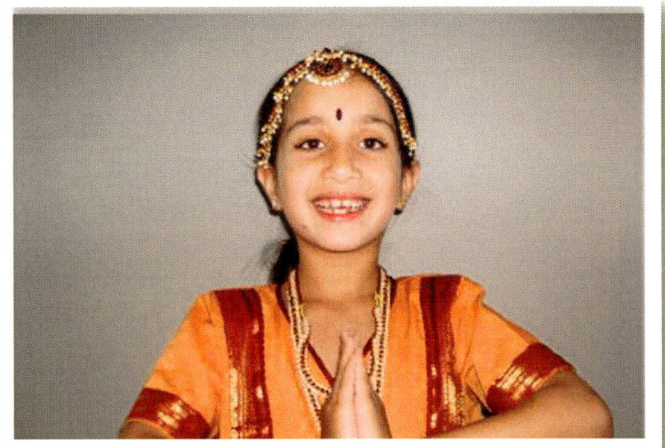
Sonali in traditional Indian costume

Sonali Speaks Three Languages

At home, Sonali's family speaks *Konkani*, their Indian language. They also speak English, which is taught in schools in India. Sonali's third language is Spanish, which she is learning in her school in Australia.

Sonali at home

Sonali at New Schools

Nandini, Sonali's mum, says that Sonali makes new friends easily, which helps a lot. One problem is that schools around the world are not all the same. In one country, Sonali was too young for grade two and had to repeat grade one.

1 *Sonali in her first year at school*

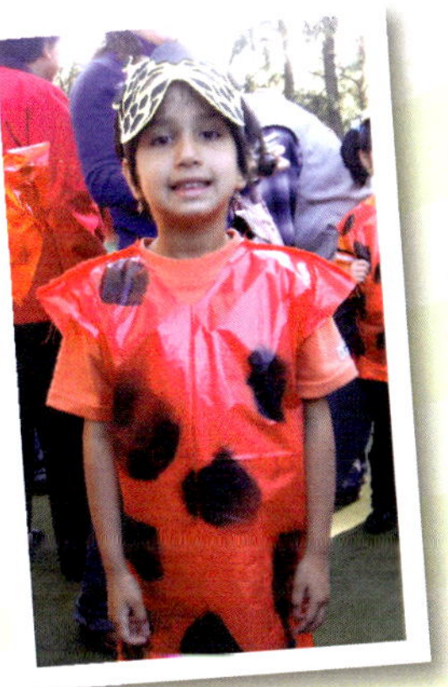

2 *Sonali in her second year at school*

3 *Sonali in her fourth year at school*

Sonali's Mum Speaks at School

Nandini likes to tell other children about their Indian culture. She has been invited to speak to Sonali's class about Diwali, the Indian Festival of Lights.

Sonali Learns Indian Dance

Sonali and her mother learn classical Indian dance. It is called *bharatanatyam*. Once, they performed this dance at Sonali's school assembly.

Sonali dances with her mother.

Sonali Plays Sports

Sonali enjoys learning new sports, such as tennis and swimming, in each new country.

Sonali learns tennis.

Sonali loves swimming classes.

A Visit Home to India

Every year, Sonali's family travel to India to visit family and friends. For people who live in other cultures, it is important to go home regularly if they can.

Sonali and her family

Social Studies

Tell the Kids First!

Nandini recounts a time when the family were preparing to leave Belgium. Sonali was four years old. Nandini and her husband thought that Sonali was too young to understand why they were moving, so they didn't tell her about it. But Sonali had overheard them talking about the move to Australia. She became very upset at school. From that time, Sonali's parents have always told both children about their next move!

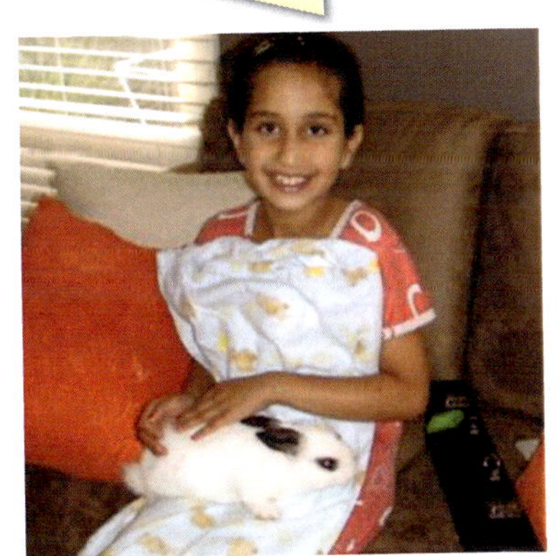

Sonali and her pet rabbit

4 Helping Families Move

Kathy Nunn

Relocation **Help** for Families

Kathy Nunn owns a relocation company. Her company helps families and pets move to new cities and countries.

Relocation Services

Their services make it easier for families to:

- find a new home
- get information about their new city or country
- pack their belongings
- move their belongings to their new city or country
- unpack their belongings in their new home
- find schools, playgroups and community services
- find a pet-travel company to transport family pets.

Why Kathy Wants to Help Families Move

Many years ago, Kathy and her family moved from the United Kingdom to Melbourne, Australia. When they arrived, they didn't know anybody. They had to learn all about their new city alone.

Now Kathy helps other new families settle into their new homes much faster and more easily.

Kathy's Family Move to Papua New Guinea

A few years after the move to Melbourne, Kathy's family had to move to PNG. Her husband got a job as an accountant for an Australian company. Kathy arranged her family's move to their new home.

A Helping Hand

Kathy's relocation company is a great help to people moving to a new place. It offers information to families, and also helps with packing and unpacking.

A friendly child welcomes Kathy's family in PNG.

Welcome to PNG!

Living in **Papua New Guinea**

While Kathy's family were in PNG, they lived in an apartment in the city of Port Moresby.

a village in PNG

A New School

While living in PNG, their two children, Andrew and Angharad, were aged four and six years old. They went to a nearby school with other expat children.

Kathy's children learnt that they could not wear their shoes inside the classroom. They left them outside the door.

EXPAT

An expat is a person who lives in a country that is not their own.

Expat is short for expatriate (ex = outside, patria = country).

Angharad's friends at her family's PNG home

Angharad in PNG

The PNG Climate

PNG has a hot, humid climate, so schools start at 7.30 am and when it's cooler, they finish early at 1.00 pm.

It gets very wet during monsoon season. Kathy remembers the heavy monsoon rains that made the dirt roads very muddy and dangerous to travel on.

Unusual Pets in Kathy's Home

Imagine the baby crocodile that lived in the family's bathtub and the little turtles on the balcony. Think about the green frogs that lived inside Kathy's apartment.

Now close your eyes and imagine what it felt like for Kathy's children to walk around with frogs on their heads!

Healthy Local Foods

Kathy bought food from the market such as taro, fish, sago and tropical fruit. Some of the foods were new and she had to learn how to cook them. One of Kathy's favourite recipes was a quiche made with eggs and ferns.

Returning Home

After two years in PNG, Kathy and her family packed up and moved back to Melbourne. Today Kathy still enjoys helping families move between countries and cities.

The Nunn family boards the plane to return to Australia.

5 A Family Moves Three Times

Sean Builds **Software**

Sean with his family in Seattle

Sean outside his office in Auckland, New Zealand

Sean is from New Zealand and is married with two daughters. He and his family have moved to different countries for work.

Sean says there are many ways to get settled in a new country:

- learn about the culture and do many of the same activities
- take part in as many community clubs and activities as possible
- buy a home and get involved in the neighbourhood
- learn the road rules – in the USA, Sean had to learn how to drive on the right (and not the left) side of the road!

Sean Loves His Job

When I met Sean in Seattle, he said, "I really love my job. People think I am stuck in a cubicle in front of my computer all day. NO! I work with lots of different people on many different software tasks."

Other reasons why Sean loves his job in IT are:

- he is always learning
- his job changes every day
- he works with people from around the world
- he travels to many countries.

Sean Works in Many Countries

Sean has worked for a software company for many years in three countries:

- New Zealand (Auckland)
- the United Kingdom (London)
- the USA (Seattle).

At Sean's job in Seattle, he manages a team of about 1200 people! The people work in different offices around the world. Sean has to travel a lot to meet his staff and their customers.

Computer Games

Sean and his team help people build software with special tools for their computers. This includes software for games, too.

Technology

Software Developers

There are over 100 million people around the world who build software for computers!

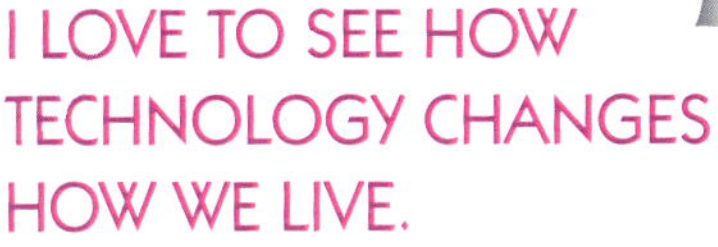

Seattle's Scenery

Sean said, "I love living in Seattle. It reminds me of my home country, New Zealand. Its green fields, mountains, lakes and rivers are beautiful, just like New Zealand!"

a New Zealand glacier river

Mt Rainier, Seattle

Social Studies and History

Bill Gates

Bill Gates is the founder of Microsoft. He lives in Seattle on Lake Washington with his family. Bill doesn't work at the company's offices anymore but is still Microsoft's chairman. He now does philanthropic work. Philanthropic work is when someone gives money and help to people in need to make their lives better or healthier.

Sean with Bill Gates in 2008

Bill Gates has made billions of dollars from his software business. For years he and his wife have given money to families in poor countries and provided funding for medical research.

6 Pets Travel, Too

Not **Without** My **Pets!**

a happy pet on the move

Pets are part of the family, so when families move to a new country, their pets often go, too. Some countries will not allow pets to enter, so sometimes people have to leave them behind with family or friends.

Pet Transport Companies and Airlines Help

Before pets travel by air, pet transport companies help people to prepare their pets for the long journey.

Airlines take extra care – pets are the last on and first off the plane.

Taking Pets to Australia

Countries have strict rules about pets coming from other parts of the world because they may spread diseases and be unwanted animals.

Bibi, the author's dog, in an air crate ready to fly

In Australia, some of the rules are below.

1. Dogs, cats and horses can come from most countries, but pet rabbits are not allowed.
2. Pets must be in quarantine for 30 days.
3. Pets must be microchipped.
4. Pets must be vaccinated.

Index

Glossary

biometric technology	Technology that measures natural features, such as eye colour, height and facial dimensions
classical	Traditional
database	A set of information, or data, about a particular subject that is stored on a computer
glacier river	A river formed from the melting of ice in a glacier, rather than a spring or rainfall
monsoon season	A season of heavy rainfall that usually occurs in areas close to the equator
quarantine	An area kept isolated from other animals in order to stop the spread of any illness
shamrock leaf	A three-leafed clover, used as the symbol of Ireland
taro	A large root vegetable, similar to a sweet potato, grown in areas in and around the Pacific